BE YOU!

For YOU!
- KN

For friends who hike mountains with me.
- ES

A STUDIO PRESS BOOK

First published in the UK in 2023 by Studio Press,
an imprint of Bonnier Books UK,
4th Floor, Victoria House, Bloomsbury Square, London WC1B 4DA
Owned by Bonnier Books,
Sveavägen 56, Stockholm, Sweden

www.bonnierbooks.co.uk

Text copyright © 2023 Karl Newson
Illustrations copyright © 2023 Ela Smietanka

1 3 5 7 9 10 8 6 4 2

Edited by Frankie Jones
Production by Giulia Caparrelli
Designed by Maddox Philpot

A CIP catalogue record for this book is available from the British Library
Printed and bound in China

BE YOU!

Karl Newson

illustrated by

Ela Smietanka

STUDIO
PRESS

Whoever
you are...

Whatever
you do...

However
you feel...

Be YOU!

If you're a...

Toucan

Tiger

Crocodile

Frog

Monkey

Elephant

Turtle

Dog

Panda

Butterfly

Peacock

Bat

Spider

Buffalo

Parrot

Cat

Wherever
you've been...

Wherever
you are...

Wherever
you go...

You're gonna go far!

Whoever
you are...

Whatever
you do...

However
you feel...

Be YOU!

If you're a...

Zebra

Octopus

Squirrel

Goose

Hedgehog

Kangaroo

Rooster

Moose

Walrus

Pangolin

Penguin

Hare

Tortoise

Pelican

Beaver

Bear

It might be hard sometimes, that's true.

There may be days you're feeling blue.

But you've got me
and I've got you...

There's nothing we can't do!

So be a...

lion

Bumblebee

HOME 100   01:90   VISITOR 90

4
PERIOD

Starfish

Whale

Wombat

Lobster

Bandicoot

Snail

Go blaze your trail!

Go shine your light!

Believe in YOU

with all your might!

You've got a **whole** world.

You've got a **big** heart.

You've got a **big** voice.

You're
tough!

You're
smart!

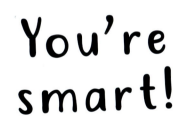

Whoever you are...

Whatever you do...

However you feel...

Be you!

Be who?
Be YOU!

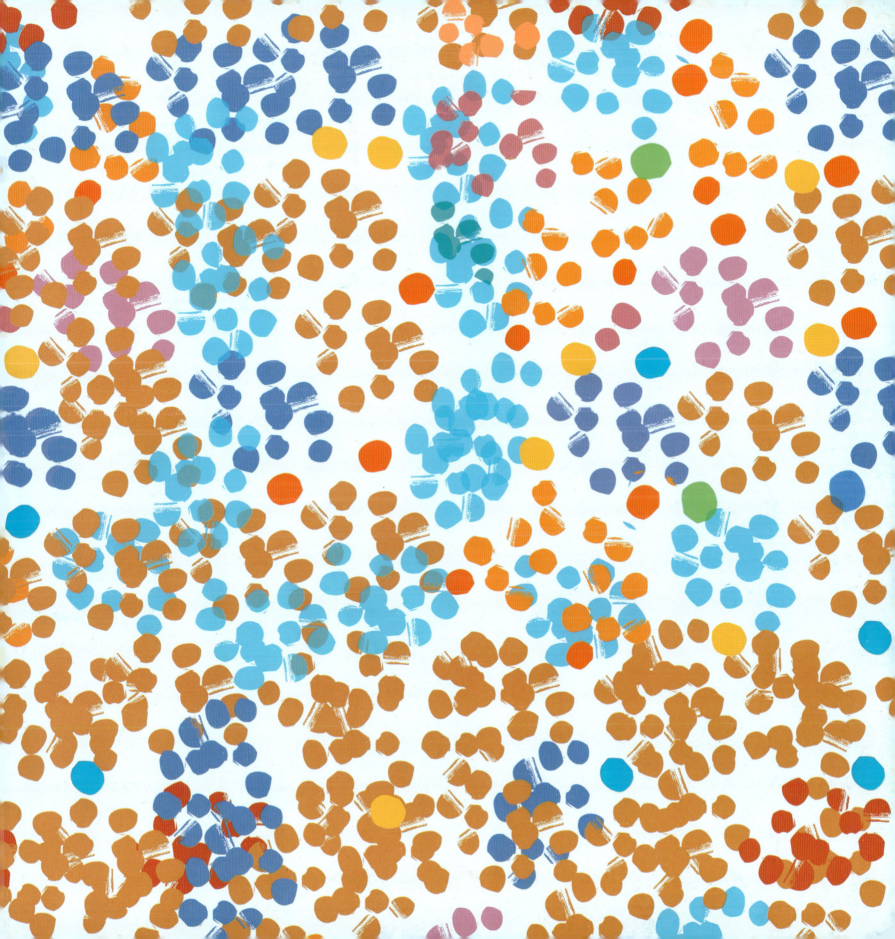